HEATHER
AND THE
STORMY BIRTHDAY

HEATHER
AND THE
STORMY BIRTHDAY

Linda Oatman High

Illustrated by
Kris Aro McLeod

KANEPRESS

AN IMPRINT OF ASTRA BOOKS FOR YOUNG READERS

New York

For three who inspire me: Connor Oatman, Dylan Bordner, and
Harper Shoun. The future is theirs. —*LOH*

For my weather guy, Peter —*KAM*

Kane Press thanks Dr. Trena Ferell from NASA Goddard Space Flight Center Earth Science
Education for reviewing the manuscript's scientific information for accuracy.

Kane Press • An imprint of Astra Books for Young Readers, • a division of
Astra Publishing House • astrapublishinghouse.com
Printed in China

Library of Congress Cataloging-in-Publication Data
Names: High, Linda Oatman, author. | McLeod, Kris Aro, illustrator.
Title: Heather and the stormy birthday / by Linda Oatman High ; illustrated by Kris Aro McLeod.
Description: First edition. | New York : Kane Press, an imprint of Astra
  Books for Young Readers, [2023] | Series: Heather whirl, weather girl |
  Audience: Ages 6-9. | Audience: Grades 2-3. | Summary: "A magical
  umbrella takes Heather and her team to experience a superstorm and help
  someone in need. Weather terms, information about ways people can
  mitigate the effects of climate change, and weather experiments
  supplement the story"-- Provided by publisher.
Identifiers: LCCN 2023005493 (print) | LCCN 2023005494 (ebook) | ISBN
  9781662670312 (hardcover) | ISBN 9781662670626 (paperback) | ISBN
  9781662670329 (ebk)
Subjects: CYAC: Magic--Fiction. | Storms--Fiction. | Weather--Fiction. |
  Helpfulness--Fiction.
Classification: LCC PZ7.H543968 Sth 2023 (print) | LCC PZ7.H543968
  (ebook) | DDC [Fic]--dc23
LC record available at https://lccn.loc.gov/2023005493
LC ebook record available at https://lccn.loc.gov/2023005494

First edition
10 9 8 7 6 5 4 3 2 1

Design by Barbara Grzeslo • Series logo design by Michelle Martinez • The text is set in
Avenir LT Std 65 Medium. • The titles are set in Avenir LT Std 65 Black.
The illustrations are based on pencil-drawn thumbnails from the illustrator's
sketchbook. She took photos of them, and transferred those to Procreate on an iPad.
The sketches became the background layer for the digital artwork in the book.

Contents

CHAPTER 1

A Gift from Nanny Pippa

It was Heather Whirl's eighth birthday. Her parents decorated all morning, hoping for a beautiful October day for the backyard party.

But the sky grew dark and windy. It started to rain. Heather's blue eyes lit up with a shade of light purple.

"Yay!" shouted Heather Whirl, twirling in circles in the yard. She threw her arms into the air, dancing.

"Rain, rain, don't go away!" she sang, as her parents chased party streamers and napkins and balloons. Heather's pets—a big hairy dog named Fog and a lizard named Blizzard—scurried about.

"This wind reminds me of the twister we had when I was a kid!" Heather's father shouted as party decorations whipped around his head. "It was wild!"

"I love wild weather!" Heather yelled, as the wind swirled the paper tablecloth above her head. "The wilder, the better!"

Twister: a tornado, waterspout, or dust devil in which the fast, circular movement of air can be seen.

Heather Whirl's birthday parties always included a weather theme. And this birthday, her eighth, was a special one. Heather's very old great-grandmother Nanny Pippa was visiting from England, and coming to her party for the first time ever.

Nanny Pippa squished into the backyard as the rain became a light mist. She used a fancy cane to help her walk, and carried a long narrow package wrapped in shiny bright paper.

"Cheerio!" called Nanny Pippa.

"She wants cereal?" whispered Heather's best friend, Edward, who had come early to help set up.

Heather laughed.

"No," she said. "That's how she says hello."

"Oh." Edward cleaned a speck on his glasses and squinted at Heather's great-grandmother.

"She's old," he whispered.

"She's literally one hundred years old," Heather
whispered back.

"What a wild, wacky, wonderful whipping wind we had
for a bit!" said Nanny Pippa. "Too bad the rain is stopping.
And here comes the sun. That's disappointing."

Nanny Pippa found a chair and plopped down.

"Happy birthday, Heather Whirl, weather girl!" she said. She motioned Heather over and whispered in her ear.

"Before your other guests arrive, we have something special in store. It's time for the magic to begin!"

Heather smiled politely. With Nanny Pippa, it was always best to pretend to understand.

Nanny Pippa held out the wrapped package.

"Hurry, unwrap it!" she said. "I don't have all the time in the world, you know."

Heather tore off the paper and opened the box. It was an umbrella! Heather loved umbrellas, and this one was especially beautiful, with a shimmery green gemstone glowing on the handle.

"It's an antique," said Nanny Pippa. "Given to me by my great-grandmother, and now given to you . . . by me!"

"That's a special gift," said Heather's mother.

"An heirloom," added Heather's father.

"Something to keep forever," said Edward.

"Thank you," said Heather. "I'm . . . gobsmacked." That was one of Nanny Pippa's British words. "It will be the most wonderful umbrella in my collection!"

"It isn't just any umbrella," said Nanny Pippa. "This umbrella holds magic."

"Magic?" asked Heather. "What kind of magic?"

Nanny Pippa patted the empty chair next to her. Heather sat down, and Nanny Pippa smiled. Fog sniffed at one of Nanny Pippa's pointy-toed boots. Blizzard crawled over the other one.

"Do you know the story of the night you were born?" she asked Heather.

"Of course," Heather replied. "I was born at midnight, and the nurse wrapped me in a soft blanket and handed me to Mom . . ."

"I mean the whole story, dear," said Nanny Pippa.

"Yes," said Heather, getting excited. "There was a big wild storm, and I had a lot of hair. It twisted and frizzed as if blown by the wind, and it stayed that way."

"That's right." Nanny Pippa turned to Heather's parents.

"And when she got older, Heather had to fall asleep to the sound of rain, or thunder, or wild, wild wind," Heather's mom said. "And I remember her favorite bedtime story was about a big flood in a Winnie-the-Pooh book! And she would never take off her rain boots, even to go to bed."

Edward snickered.

"You did that?" he whispered.

Heather shrugged.

"I loved rain boots," she said. "I still love rain boots."

"And remember how she said in kindergarten that she was a meteorologist?" Nanny Pippa went on. "Her teacher was so impressed that she knew such a big word."

Meteorologist: a weather forecaster or an expert on weather.

"Of course I knew that word—from *The Big Books of Weather*, volumes one to five!" Heather ran her hands through her wild hair, taming it away from her face. "But what about the *magic*, Nanny Pippa?" she asked, trying to be patient.

"You'll find out, just as I did," said Nanny Pippa with a mysterious wink.

Fog let out a sudden bark and Blizzard scurried up Heather's arm to her shoulder.

And then Heather Whirl, Weather Girl, noticed something.

The bright green gemstone blinked fast and frantic, flashing a glaring light from the antique umbrella's handle.

CHAPTER 2
A Blinking Green Gem

Heather looked at her pets and her friend Edward, who all stared wide-eyed at the umbrella.

Nanny Pippa's eyes flashed silver. "Quickly, quickly!" she said to Heather's parents. "Time for your other presents. Heather's first adventure is about to begin!"

Heather opened the gifts from her parents, which included a special waterproof Weather Journal and a phone with Wi-Fi so that Heather could research weather.

"Now," said Nanny Pippa. "I think you'll know what to do. Are you going alone . . . or bringing a team?" She patted Fog on the head.

Heather raised the umbrella, popping it up with a swish. Rain began to fall once again. Blizzard and Fog curled around her. Edward stepped forward and took her free hand. "We've been best friends for eight years, ever since we were babies," he said. "Whatever's happening, I'm in."

The four adventurers huddled together beneath the umbrella. Nanny Pippa giggled.

The green gemstone flashed and sparkled. Heather pressed it firmly.

Her entire body twisted. Swirling, whirling, twirling fast as a human tornado, Heather flew high into the sky. So did Edward, and Blizzard, and Fog. It was wild and wonderful and weird, and Heather's heart flipped.

Heather blinked, and then landed gently on a sand dune, along with Edward and her pets.

The four looked at one another, stunned, eyes wide with shock and confusion. A storm raged. Wind whipped. Rain pounded down. Thunder roared like a monster. Ocean waves, angry and high, crashed before their eyes. Heavy dark clouds hovered over the ocean.

"What a ride!" Heather shouted into the wind. Her hair was wilder than ever.

Edward stared up at the ominous sky, then down at the ground. "Ugh," he said, "My shoes are getting dirty. Look at all this wet sand!"

"The magic brought us here . . . but where are we?" asked Heather. She wiped rainwater from her eyes.

"The East Coast of the United States," said a tiny voice coming from Heather's shoulder.

She gasped. "Blizzard! You're . . . talking!"

"What did you expect?" said a deeper voice from near Heather's knees. "Like the lady said, it's magic!" Fog nudged Heather with his wet nose. "Now, what do you think is happening here?"

Heather thought for a minute, gazing at the waves and the sky. The beach went on for miles, with a few houses above the sandy shore. Trees whipped in the wind.

"Here's my hypothesis," she said. "That means here is my scientific idea. I believe that we are in a superstorm."

"It's definitely a *super* storm," agreed Fog. "Wowie zowie!"

"Hey, this is super-cool! A superstorm is a totally rare event." Blizzard read from Heather's new phone, holding it between his claws.

"A superstorm is a strong storm that covers an unusually large area," the lizard read. "It's not a hurricane. It's not a tsunami. But it can be destructive and dangerous."

Tsunami: a large, sometimes destructive wave, often caused by an earthquake.

The dog grinned, slobbery tongue hanging out as he looked over Blizzard's shoulder. "Dude, it can be like a thousand miles wide? That's rad!" said Fog.

"Ooh!" said Heather. "When we get home, I can write about this in my new Weather Journal!"

"Yikes!" squeaked Blizzard. "Any wild weather sounds scary to me! I don't care what you call it!"

"Don't be so afraid, bud," Fog said. "You're a lizard, not a chicken."

Heather and Edward stared at one another, and then began to laugh. They laughed and laughed. Wind whipped around them, and rain splattered beneath the protection of the umbrella, making their faces cold and wet.

"Wow," said Edward. "It's so cold. I hope we don't get sick from this."

"This is amazing!" said Heather. "Wilder than a windstorm! Twistier than a twister! Is this really happening? Am I dreaming?"

"We're not dreaming," said Edward. "I can taste the salt. And, Heather, your eyes are a color I've never seen. Like gray mixed with green and black, with tiny yellow stars."

Edward shivered. "How did we get here? And what if we never get back?"

"The umbrella got us here," said Heather. "It will take us back home. And I have a feeling it will help protect us."

"What if you lose the umbrella?" asked Edward.

"I won't." Heather clutched the handle of the umbrella tightly.

She looked at her friends. Edward's glasses fogged, and his face streamed with rain. Blizzard's tiny claws sunk into wet sand. Fog's fur stood up in wet spikes.

"We got this!" she shouted.

"We got this!" yelled Edward.

The animals joined in, howling and chirping into the wind.

The four gave each other high fives, which were actually low fives, so that Fog and Blizzard could reach Heather's and Edward's hands.

"From now on, I'm calling myself something more than just a weather expert," said Heather. "More than a junior meteorologist. More than a climate scientist in training. I am now . . . an *investigator* of weather! I am . . . Heather Whirl, Weather Girl."

Edward pulled out his phone.

"The official team photographer is going to take some pictures, so that we all remember this day and everything we learned," Edward said. He clicked pictures of Heather Whirl, the animals, the ocean, and the sky. Then he took a selfie of all four friends.

Fog's big pink tongue rolled out of his mouth, and he panted.

"Dude, I hope I look okay," said the dog. "My fur's kind of a mess."

"Don't be so vain," squeaked Blizzard. "You're a dog. You always look like a dog."

"I have a feeling the magic has a mission for us," said Heather. "So let's find out what it is!"

Just down the beach a bit, TV cameras filmed a weather reporter who swayed in the wind, trying to keep his footing. A red bowtie blew from his neck and tumbled down the beach. Heather and Edward giggled.

"Grab your tie, dude," said Fog. "A superstorm is a dress-up occasion."

"He might be a meteorologist," Heather said with excitement. "Let's go talk to him!"

The group of four trudged up the beach. Ocean water washed over their feet, and they sunk into the sand. The water pulled strong, and it drew them to the left. They sunk deeper. Edward let out a panicked yelp.

"Don't worry, Edward," said Heather. "I got this. You're in the backwash. We can pull you out."

Edward's eyes widened.

"Backwash?! What's that?" he gasped.

"It's the strong pull of the water as waves run back down the shore," Heather explained.

Heather held out the handle of the umbrella to Edward.

"Grab on," she said. "I'll pull you out. With help from the umbrella."

Edward grasped the umbrella handle, and Heather lifted her feet from the wet sand, stepping back. Edward sank deeper, and the umbrella handle slipped from his hands.

"Help," he gasped.

CHAPTER 3

Somebody or Something Needs Help

"Stay calm," said Heather. "I've got you, Edward. Grab the handle again. Don't let go."

Edward grasped the umbrella handle, holding tight. Fog pushed him from behind. Blizzard tried to dig wet sand away from Edward's feet.

"Bro, that's not doing any good," barked Fog. "Just help to push him, but don't sink."

Blizzard's tiny eyes narrowed with fright as the water pulled him to the left. "Holy guacamole!" the lizard squeaked. "I'm in the undertow!"

"The undertow is out farther, bud," barked Fog.

Undertow:
the pull of the water away
from shore, out where
the waves break.

"Don't you remember Heather reading to us from *Marine Meteorology*? This is backwash because we're still on the beach!"

"Just keep swimming, Blizzard," yelled Heather.

Heather gave the handle a big yank. She pulled Edward to drier sand. Edward collapsed on the ground, catching his breath.

Blizzard frantically paddled in the water, and Fog ran to the lizard, splashing water with his huge paws.

Fog lifted Blizzard from the wet sand with his mouth, then nudged Edward until he stood up. The four friends moved away from the dangerous ocean waters. They trudged back toward a row of homes that lined the upper edges of the sand.

Nobody else was outdoors . . . just the news crew, Edward, Heather, and her pets.

"That was terrifying!" gasped Edward. "And look at my shoes."

"Yikes," squeaked Blizzard.

The four huddled together, catching their breath.

"Calm your hearts," said Heather.

"Mine is pounding like the waves," said Edward in a trembly voice.

"Mine is flying around like the wind," said Blizzard.

"My heart is like thunder," panted Fog.

"It's okay now," said Heather. "We're safe."

They looked down the beach at the news crew. They were still filming. They looked back at the houses. A few people peered out of windows.

Then there was a sound, a small, high-pitched sound coming from the direction of the houses.

"Help," said a voice. The sound seemed to be coming from a lime-green house built high upon pilings.

"Why is that house up on wooden stilts?" asked Edward.

"Houses near the beach are often built high," explained Heather. "Those are called pilings. It's one thing that people can do to protect themselves and their homes when they live near the ocean. Sand dunes and other things can help too."

Then they heard another sound from the green house: a desperate high screech.

"That sounded like a cat, dudes," said Fog. "A cat in danger."

"It wasn't a meow," argued Blizzard.

"Help," called the voice again.

"We've got to go," Heather said. "Somebody, or some*thing*, needs help."

"What if it's, like, some terrifying mean sea creature washed up from the superstorm?" asked Edward.

"Your imagination is way too vivid, bro," said Fog.

"HELP!" the voice trilled even higher, even louder, joined by the scary screeching sounds.

"I . . . have goose bumps," Edward said.

"I have lizard bumps," said Blizzard.

"Get a grip," said Heather. "Somebody needs help, and we are the only ones out here."

"HELP! HELP! HELP! HELP!" shouted the voice.

CHAPTER 4

Star of the Storm

The group of four hurried toward the sound of the voice, the wind lashing them as they ran as fast as they could through the rain-drenched sand.

"Weather Girl to the rescue!" panted Heather. "A climate scientist in training will save the day!"

"This better be a good idea," Edward said. "It could be dangerous."

"You worry too much," growled Fog.

"The sounds are coming from that little green house." Heather pointed. "Right there."

They ran to the front door. Heather knocked. Edward knocked, too. Fog barked. Blizzard scurried up the door frame and rang the bell. No answer.

Heather tried the doorknob. It was unlocked.

"HELP!" squealed the voice.

Heather looked at her friends. She opened the door. An elderly lady lay on the floor by a sofa. A big gray cat peered out from under it.

"Help!" said the lady. "My cat was hiding from the storm, and I fell when I tried to help him."

"Are you hurt?" asked Heather.

"No," said the woman. "I just have very old bones— osteoporosis. I have trouble getting up. I need someone to help me, but I live alone. My nurse is coming late today because of the storm."

Heather knelt down beside the lady.

"Don't worry," she said. "We know what to do, because my Nanny Pippa falls sometimes, and my parents taught us the safe way to help older people get back up when they fall."

Heather and Edward went to the kitchen. They each

picked up a chair and carried it to the living room. They put a chair on each side of the lady.

"Okay," Heather said to the lady. "We'll keep the chairs steady, and we'll be here to make sure you don't lose your balance and fall down again."

The lady nodded.

"I've done this with my caregiver several times," she said.

"Just take it slow," Heather said. "Take your time and you'll be fine. We've got you."

The lady took a big breath, and then put a hand on each chair. She carefully and shakily raised herself. Edward and Heather made sure that the chairs didn't move.

"Good job!" Heather said, as the lady slowly raised to a standing position.

"Teamwork makes the dream work," Edward said.

"Have a seat on the sofa," Heather said to the woman.

Fog licked the lady's hand and Blizzard skittered out of the way.

Heather and Edward walked on each side of the lady, their hands gently placed on her arms.

Heather helped the lady to lower herself slowly onto the sofa. The cat darted out from under the sofa and curled up in the woman's lap.

"Problem solved," panted Fog, backing away from the cat. "I'm not a big fan of cats, though, so I'll just keep my distance."

"It's only a cat!" squeaked Blizzard. The cat purred.

"Am I dreaming?" said the lady. "I could swear I hear these animals talking. Maybe I hit my head when I fell."

Heather just smiled.

"Weird things happen during superstorms," she said. "Just like magic."

"Thank you," said the lady. "Thank you so much. You saved us."

"*Bowwow woof!*" said Fog, shooting Heather a wink.

A knock came from the door, which still swung open. It was the news crew.

"Is everything okay?" asked the reporter. "We heard shouting, and saw you all running, and then you just disappeared into this house."

"Everything is fine," said Heather. "Just fine. This lady fell and we helped her up. But I think someone should stay with her until her nurse gets here."

"He should arrive any minute now," the woman said.

"We're happy to wait," said the news reporter. Then he smiled. "And while we do . . . we saw you and the animals help your friend here out of the water. It was an amazing and brave rescue, and we'd like to interview you on camera for our news report. You'll be the star of the storm."

Heather grinned.

"Cool," she said.

"She should fix her hair and brush off some of the sand," Edward said.

"Don't worry," said the reporter. "We are in the middle of a storm!"

"A *super*storm!" said Heather.

The cameras pointed at Heather. The reporter held the microphone before Heather Whirl.

"My name is Heather Whirl, and I'm eight. Eight today! I'm a wild weather girl—I mean, a climate scientist in training. I'm learning about how climate change makes wild weather happen. We got here by magic—"

Edward dug his elbow into Heather's ribs and she jumped.

"Right! I mean, we got here by *luck*, just in time to help someone out in the middle of this superstorm."

"You seem to know a lot about today's weather," said the reporter.

"Here's what I know about this storm that's happening. Like many superstorms, it probably started with a tropical wave in the Caribbean. And it developed into a tropical storm, one that covers an extremely large area. Scientists say that that climate change may make storms worse."

"That's a big problem," said the reporter. "What do you think we should do about it?"

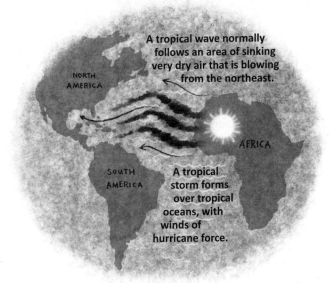

A tropical wave normally follows an area of sinking very dry air that is blowing from the northeast.

NORTH AMERICA

AFRICA

SOUTH AMERICA

A tropical storm forms over tropical oceans, with winds of hurricane force.

"I'm on a mission to learn about extreme weather so people understand why we need to help the Earth," Heather said. "And we also need to help people who get stuck in wild weather. My three friends here are my dream team. After we get home, I'm going to find out more about superstorms. It'll be even more exciting now that I've been *in* one!"

At the end of the interview, everyone clapped. Heather was the star of the storm!

They all shook hands (and paws and claws).

"Heather Whirl, Weather Girl to the rescue!" said the reporter.

37

Heather noticed the gemstone on her umbrella pulsing with warm light.

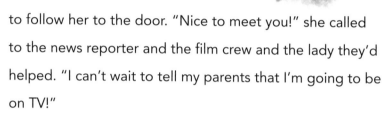

"It's getting dark outside," Heather said. "It's time for us to go back home."

She motioned for her friends to follow her to the door. "Nice to meet you!" she called to the news reporter and the film crew and the lady they'd helped. "I can't wait to tell my parents that I'm going to be on TV!"

They waved.

"Get home safely!" they all called.

"Oh, we will, I promise!"

Heather closed the door behind them and popped up the umbrella. She gathered her friends and pressed her finger to the gemstone.

Heather's entire body twisted. Swirling, whirling, twirling fast as a human tornado, Heather and her friends raised high into the sky.

CHAPTER 5
The Party Goes On

In the blink of an eye, they dropped gently into Heather's backyard, where the weather was ordinary October weather: a bit cool. No superstorm.

And all her party guests had arrived. "Happy birthday, Heather!" they shouted.

Heather and her friends shook sand from their hair and fur.

"This cake looks absolutely delicious!" said Nanny Pippa. "And I think it's about time we have some." She lowered her voice and leaned in toward Heather. "How was your first wild weather journey?"

"We were . . . gobsmacked," whispered Heather. Her eyes had returned to their normal color of calm blue.

"Heather was the star of a superstorm," said Edward.

He examined his shoes, wiping away some of the sand. "And we all learned a lot."

"Hooray for Heather Whirl, Weather Girl!" said Nanny Pippa, as Heather lowered the umbrella.

Heather's mother lit eight candles on the cloud-shaped cake.

"Make a wish!" Mom said, and Heather Whirl closed her eyes.

She blew out all eight candles with one big breath, a puff of air like a gust of wind. Edward fished his phone from his pocket and took a picture.

After all the cake had been eaten and the other guests had gone home, Edward came over to sit by Heather.

"What did you wish?" asked Edward, dabbing his face with a napkin to clean up a tiny bit of icing. He brushed cake crumbs from his lap.

"I can't tell my wish, or it won't come true," said Heather. Her eyes flashed a rainbow of colors. From across the yard, Nanny Pippa grinned.

"This was the most magical birthday ever," said Heather. "And now here we are—back to normal, on a normal old ordinary day with normal weather. I can't wait to write in my Weather Journal!"

That night, Heather wrote slowly and carefully, neatly recording all that she'd experienced on the adventure.

There was so much to learn, so much to do . . . and Heather couldn't wait for the next wild weather adventure.

Heather and the Wildfires

It was a gray day in November, clouds hanging heavy and dark. Heather and Edward were helping Heather's father to bake cookies when Heather's eye color suddenly changed from their normal blue to a dark purple splattered with drops of red and slashes of green.

Edward stared at her.

"Uh-oh," said Edward. "Your eyes changed color. Here we go again."

A light in the room caught their attention. Edward and Heather both looked at Heather's special umbrella, standing in a corner by the door. Fog ran to the umbrella and sniffed it. Blizzard skittered to the dog's side.

The gem on the handle of the umbrella flashed frantically.

Heather turned off the cookie mixer. Edward spilled some honey on the floor and his shoes.

"Oh, no!" he said. "My new shoes! Plus, I have flour all over my shirt."

"No time to worry about your shoes or your shirt," said Heather. "It's time for another adventure."

Edward squished quickly across the kitchen floor, following Heather to the umbrella. Heather's pets looked up at her.

"Come on!" said Heather. "Bye, Dad!"

"Be safe!" Heather's father shouted as Heather picked up the umbrella. The four friends hurried outside into the chilly gray November day. Heather popped up the umbrella and pressed the gemstone.

Heather's entire body twisted, along with the umbrella. Swirling, whirling, twirling fast as a human tornado, Heather flew high into the sky. So did Edward, and Blizzard, and Fog. It was wild and crazy and weird, just like the first time, and Heather's heart flipped exactly as it had on her last wild weather adventure.

Heather blinked, and her body landed gently upon the

ground, her three friends dropping down beside her. The smell of smoke hung thick in the air, and all four of them began to cough.

"Holy guacamole!" squeaked Blizzard. "Look!"

The lizard pointed into the distance, towards high hills. The hills flamed with fire.

"Dude!" said Fog. "We're in California! The West Coast of America."

"How do you know?" asked Edward. He lifted one shoe after another, still examining the mess of sticky honey.

"Um, that sign over there." Fog lifted a paw, pointing.

Heather's Weather Journal
Superstorms

I'm superexcited to begin this new project that I'm calling Heather's Weather Journal! I think it'll be good for me to keep track of things I learn, and also maybe I can use all this information in my future career.

So here goes.

My wild weather adventure happened on the East Coast of the US in a superstorm. A superstorm is a storm all in its own category: it's not a hurricane, which is a tropical cyclone with very high winds. It's not a tsunami, which is a long, high wave or set of waves often caused by earthquakes. A superstorm is nontropical, which means it's not somewhere near the equator, like the Caribbean. A superstorm is a very wild and very windy event, and it usually includes lots of rain. One thing that makes it a superstorm is the extremely large area that it affects. Superstorms are big deals!

Superstorm is a pretty new term. One of the first superstorms might have been a big storm of 1880 that hit the northwestern United States. Back then, it was called "The Great Gale." That storm came from the tropics and did a lot of damage. The fact that the wind and rain caused so much destruction made it a superstorm. I bet it would have been scary to experience.

Superstorm Sandy was the most dangerous and destructive storm of the 2012 hurricane season. It started as a hurricane in the end of October, and the storm ended as a superstorm in the beginning of November! The storm affected a big area: all the way from the Caribbean to Canada.

Superstorm Sandy caused more than 70 billion dollars in damage, and over 200 people actually died. Homes and businesses were destroyed, and it took a long time for people to rebuild. But, like my own team, people worked together to make things better! We can do a lot when we work with our squad.

Now that my friends and I have been in a superstorm, I

hope that fewer of these kinds of storms happen. I also really hope that people are better prepared for superstorms, so that everybody stays safe. This is why it is important for people all over the world to work together to make our Earth better. Superstorm is a good word for the kind of storm that we experienced on our magical journey. It was a very unusual and powerful storm, and it was superinteresting. It was also a little bit scary, so we were all happy to return home safe and sound!

Edward's Weather Photos

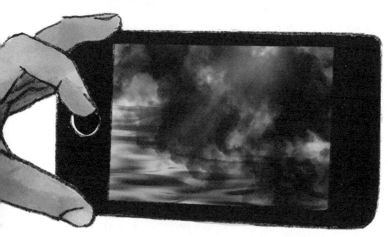

Notes from Blizzard

I might be a lizard but I'm great at research! I learned that superstorms may be caused by climate change. To understand climate change, human people, it's important to first understand the meaning of climate. Climate is the big picture of weather in a certain area of Earth, and it includes superinteresting things like temperature and rainfall amounts from year to year. "Climate change" is the change that is happening to climate all over Earth, and that affects us lizards as well as other animals and people.

The part of climate change that is most creepy to me is that the Earth is getting hotter than scientists have ever seen. Some people call this "global warming." Yikes!

The warming is caused by something called "the greenhouse effect," and holy flying insects, it's confusing, but I'll try to explain. A greenhouse helps plants grow by holding in warmth. And Earth has its own sort of greenhouse: the atmosphere. The "greenhouse gases" high above Earth include carbon dioxide and methane, which create a shield around the Earth and act like a greenhouse.

So rays from the sun pass through this shield to warm the Earth. The Earth shoots heat back into outer space. The greenhouse gases stop heat from escaping, keeping the Earth warm. More gases make the Earth warmer—and it could get too warm.

We lizards are cold-blooded so we rely on our environment to warm our bodies up to just the right temperature. We don't need global warming or climate change in our lives . . . Yikes!

Things that people can do to help reduce the gases are to walk, or ride bicycles, more often, reducing use of cars. You humans can recycle. You can turn off lights and screens that are not being used. Every teeny-tiny little bit helps!

It's also up to the big companies to help our planet. They can do things like reduce use of fossil fuels, and also figure out how to use more environmentally friendly energy. We can help convince them to do these things by emailing them and writing letters. Big companies are made up of lots of human beings, and all humans need to care about the Earth.

So, kids, send those emails! Write those letters! Make phone calls! Every voice matters, and you all rock!

Fog's Tips and Advice

We dogs like to be helpers, and we are all about protecting human beings, so here are some of my best tips and advice for humans.

There are things people can do to protect themselves from superstorms when they live near the ocean. And speaking of the ocean, I really love running in it! The salt water feels so good on my paws.

Humans can use natural barriers like sand dunes and reefs to keep rising water from their houses. Keep those homes safe, doggone it!

They can build their houses high on stilts called pilings. These are paws-itively brilliant for protection!

They can evacuate when necessary, which means that they leave their home and retreat to higher ground. Go as fast as a dog fetching a stick! Nobody wants to leave home, but sometimes you have to in order to stay safe. So when you hear the order to evacuate, hit the road and get out of town.

When the weather forecasts say that a big storm is coming, it is a good idea for people to stock up on food and water. And don't forget the dog kibble. Bone appétit!

They can also be sure to have batteries for flashlights. And batteries can power a radio, so people can hear emergency warnings even if the electricity is out. You need light to see where to find our dog treats.

They can charge their cell phones before the storm hits. Humans love texting and talking, you know. Blah-blah-blah, bark! But they can get warnings on their cell phones too!

People should have whatever medical supplies they might need, like medicines and other things. The lady we helped in the green house had a condition called osteoporosis, so she might have needed medication for that.

Some people put wooden boards over their windows before the storm arrives in order to protect the glass from breaking. Don't have a ruff day—protect your windows!

I hope that my tips help to keep humans safe. Weather forecasts often give people enough time to prepare for the big storms . . . which is a good thing.

STAY SAFE, DUDES AND DUDETTES!

Activities, Riddles, and More

Heather here. I'm so happy that my animal friends are big on helping out. One thing that I like to do to help me learn and understand is to experiment and try activities. Here are some that I tried. My parents helped with Rain in a Jar.

Rain in a Jar

You will need an adult to help with this.

Materials needed:

A glass jar

A plate

water

ice cubes

Have an adult heat water until it is steaming. Carefully pour the hot water into the jar until it is about $1/3$ filled. Put the plate over the top of the jar and wait a minute or two. Put ice cubes on top of the plate and watch closely to see what happens inside the jar. Streaks of water will run down the sides of the jar. You have made it rain inside the jar.

The cold plate caused the warm air inside the jar to condense and form water droplets. This is the same thing that happens in the atmosphere when it rains: warm moist air rises and meets colder air high in the atmosphere. The water vapor condenses and forms moisture that falls to the ground in the form of rain.

How to Find Wind Speed by Observation

The only materials you need for this observation are your eyes! You use a tool called the Beaufort scale, invented in 1805 by a navy officer in Britain. It was invented long ago, and it's still used today!

Here's the chart for the Beaufort scale. Try estimating wind speed with it on the next breezy or stormy day. You could even make a wind journal to keep track over a period of several weeks or months.

Beaufort Scale

Beaufort Number	Wind Speed (mph)	Seamen's Term	Effects on Land
0	under 1	Calm	Smoke rises vertically.
1	1–4	Light air	Smoke drift indicates wind direction; wind vanes do not move.
2	4–7	Light breeze	Wind felt on face; leaves rustle; wind vanes begin to move.
3	8–12	Gentle breeze	Leaves, small twigs in constant motion; light flags extend.
4	13–18	Moderate breeze	Dust, leaves, and loose paper rise up; small branches move.
5	19–24	Fresh breeze	Small trees begin to sway.
6	25–31	Strong breeze	Large branches of trees in motion; whistling heard in wires.
7	32–38	Moderate gale	Whole trees in motion; resistance felt in walking against the wind.
8	39–46	Fresh gale	Twigs and small branches break off trees
9	47–54	Strong gale	Slight structural damage occurs; slate blown from roofs
10	55–63	Whole gale	Trees break.
11	64–72	Storm	Widespread damage.
12	73 or higher	Hurricane force	Violence and destruction.

Funny Business

Wild weather can be serious and scary, so I like to use jokes and riddles to lighten the mood. Laughing is a good thing, and it helps to chill out sometimes. Here are some weather jokes that crack me up.

What does a cloud wear under its raincoat?
Thunderwear!

What did one lightning bolt say to the other?
You shock me!

What did one hurricane say to another?
I have my eye on you!

Heather's Favorite
Weather Websites

Weather and Climate, NASA Climate Kids:

climatekids.nasa.gov/menu/weather-and-climate/

NASA has observed that the Earth's climate is becoming warmer, and this website informs readers about the difference between weather and climate and NASA missions that study weather and climate. The site contains information for both educators/parents and kids, along with games, activities, and videos.

National Weather Service (NWS) Education:

weather.gov/education/

This website from the National Weather Service contains a wealth of weather resources for adults and children alike. From science to safety to outreach activities, the NWS provides lots of information about weather and climate. Readers can explore future career opportunities in the field, and connect with local meteorologists.

National Oceanic and Atmospheric Administration (NOAA):

noaa.gov/educational-resources

Offers online games such as *Save Our Beach* and *Recycle City*. Kids can find plenty of fun education resources on the site.

Severe Weather 101:

nssl.noaa.gov/education/svrwx101/

The National Severe Storms Laboratory invites readers to step into the wild world of weather.

NWS Weather 101 Classes:

weather.gov/wrn/weather-101-classes

The National Weather Service offers YouTube links from which viewers can learn about wild weather around the world.

About the Author

Linda Oatman High is an experienced and versatile children's book author of more than 25 books for children (and teens), including picture books, middle-grade readers, and YA novels. Her work includes *Hound Heaven*, which was nominated for the Rebecca Caudill Award; *City of Snow: The Great Blizzard of 1888*, which was added to the 2005 NCSS Notable Social Studies Trade Book list; and many others. Linda holds an MFA from Vermont College in writing for children and young adults, and teaches both nationally and internationally. Visit lindaoatmanhigh.com.

About the Illustrator

Kris Aro McLeod is an author, illustrator, and former school art teacher. She has illustrated several children's books, including *The Peculiar Haunting of Thelma Bee*, *Catch a Kiss*, and *Lizzy and the Last Day of School*. She has illustrated and written poems for *Ladybug*, *Spider*, and *Cricket* magazines. Her work has been reviewed in *School Library Journal*, *Kirkus Reviews*, and others. Visit krisaromcleod.com.